A Twin's Revenge
A Short Story

CHONTAE COOK

A Twin's Revenge
Copyright © 2022 Chontae Cook

Table of Contents

A Twin's Revenge

Chapter 1

In Georgia, on the east side, at 9:45am, on a rainy November day in the year 2000, we came two months early. My name was Harlem, and I had an identical twin named Honesty. I was two minutes older. When I said we looked exactly alike, everything from head to toe, birthmarks and all; you couldn't tell us apart.

Our mom's name was Halley. She was a doctor, and our dad, Watson, was a correctional officer at the state prison. We entered this world having a great life. Both parents were perfect; we did everything together until we got older.

When me and my sister were nine, our mom and dad started arguing all the time. Sometimes we would get sent to our room, and a couple minutes later Mom would be crying and Dad shouting. The door would open and close, then we knew Dad had left out. We would go running to Mom, asking if she was okay. She would say, *"Yes, but don't ever let a man disrespect you or put his hands on you, do you understand?"*

We would say yes, and she said, *"No matter what, always protect each other."*

We would say okay and hold her.

Our father would come back later that day or in the morning like nothing happened. We would be leaving out for school and Mom would be heading out the door for work. She was a good person; kind, loving and had a good heart. She always made sure me and Honesty were well taken care of. We had a good relationship with Dad too, until we noticed the way he started treating Mom and calling her out her name. We were at that age to understand. Sometimes they were okay together, we would hear them making love, and then there were times where all you would hear was arguing. Mom would say, *"You need to stop drinking!"*

Dad would respond, *"Woman, it's my damn money!"*

She would say, *"Who you been laying up with, what's her name?"*

Dad would say, *"None of your damn business."* He didn't have to explain shit to nobody, he was a grown ass man. He could fuck whoever he wanted.

He was cheating on our mom. She knew, and so did we.

Our father was known as the man in Georgia, he had a lot of women fans. He had a good job and a beautiful royal blue Cadillac he would show off in, cruising up and down the street. This went on for years. It was even rumored that he had other kids floating around. My mom didn't care. She was a strong woman. It probably bothered her, but she had to be strong for me and Honesty, who we called Hon.

Honesty had a heart like Mom. She would give you anything: her very last, food, money, advice. I was the tough one. I wasn't taking no shit. My heart was good too, but when it came to my mom and sister, I took a different turn.

As we got older, the arguing and lovemaking went on and off.

Chapter 2

WE had just turned fifteen. It was a Saturday morning. Me and Honesty woke up and Mom was in her room in tears. Dad had given her a bruise underneath her eye. He put his hands on her and I was mad as hell. He wasn't there; he left before we woke up. We asked what happened.

Mom was always straight with us. "Your father got mad because he said it was time I obeyed him. I told him I'm not his child, I'm his wife. He said what he says goes, and I disagreed. He smacked me."

Honesty said, "Mom, he has to go. He can't be here. He is always hurting you with the name calling, and now hitting you."

I said, "Not to mention the cheating."

Mom said, "But he loves you girls."

I said, "No he doesn't, not when he's hurting our mother." I walked out to get Mom something for her eye, and Honesty decided to make breakfast: bacon, eggs, and toast.

We sat in Mom's big bed and watched *Good Times* until Mom cut it off and told us to look at her. She said, "Do y'all remember what I told you when you girls were nine?"

We said yes.

She said, "Harlem, tell me one thing I tell you every year."

I said, "Never let a man disrespect you."

She said, "Honesty, tell me something."

Hon said, "Never let any man put his hands on you; that kind of relationship, get out of!"

We both said, "And we have to protect each other always."

Mom said, "The name calling, the putting you down, that's abuse. Also, you don't need it, do you understand?"

We said yes.

"Mom, is something wrong?" I asked.

"No. I want y'all to promise me that y'all are going to finish school and go to college. I want you to be ready for the world out there because we have some cruel people living in it."

"Promise," we said in unison.

"Okay, we ate and had our talk. Now let's go shopping."

Honesty said, "But your eye!"

"That's nothing some shades can't fix."

We laughed, got up and dressed, and a girl's day it was. We shopped, ate lunch, went to the movies, and enjoyed every bit of it until we got home and Dad was there.

We walked in, and Mom took her bags to the room.

He said, "Girls, your dad don't get no kiss?"

Honesty said, "Sure," and kissed him on the cheek.

I kept it moving and went in my room.

He said, "Harlem!"

I came out of the room, looked him in his face, and said, "Why would you hit our mother?"

Mom was shocked.

Honesty grabbed my hand.

Dad said, "It's grown up stuff you wouldn't understand."

I said, "I understand a male is not supposed to hit a female. Women should be treated like a queen and with respect."

He froze, and his face went through a range of emotions before it settled on shame. "You're right. I apologize for hitting your mom, my wife, and it won't happen again. But you need to stay in a child's place."

I walked off, rolling my eyes, and Honesty followed.

I heard him telling Mom he was sorry. "Harlem is going to be a tough one. She's not going to take no shit."

Mom said, "Yes, she's going to be Honesty's protector."

Chapter 3

My parents stayed together. They had their ups and down, arguments and sex, until Mom got tired of his shit and asked for a divorce.

Three years later, when we were eighteen, Mom asked Dad to leave because the house was hers. He didn't care, he had a whole bunch of hoes claiming he was their baby daddy.

Me, Mom and Hon stayed in the house.

Most of the time, Honesty was with her so-called boyfriend, Rome, who she hooked up with. Rome was much older than her. He had her by twelve years, but Mom didn't know, and he was a dealer.

I also had a friend, a female, and her name was Cali. She was twenty three years old, a nurse from across the way. I told my mom about her.

I was Bi; I liked them both. Love was love, as long as you treated me right, I would treat you right.

Mom said, "Follow your heart."

That was what I loved about her. She was always understanding. She knew Honesty was seeing someone. She might have understood the age difference, but the part she was not going to like was that he was a dealer. That was a big *no* in this family.

We were both going to college. I was going for law, and I boxed at the gym in my spare time. Honesty was going to be a physical therapist.

We stuck with our promise of finishing school.

Mom was so proud that day, seeing us walk across the stage at our high school graduation. Dad too. He visited us a lot. He and Mom remained friends because of us. He would come over wanting to eat and watch movies, and Mom would let him. There was still a little love there.

One night, me and Hon came home from the club and walked in on them having sex. That was something we didn't want to see, but Mom had to get hers too.

The next morning, Honesty had class. Dad stayed the night. He came in my room and said, "Harlem, I know we're not on good terms, but no matter what, I'm still your father and I love y'all. I know I made some mistakes, but I do apologize."

"I understand, and I love you too, Dad."

He said, "I need you to do me a favor. You know that chump Honesty is dealing with named Rome?"

I stared at him, wondering where he was going with this. "I've seen him around but never met him."

"He's a dealer and known for putting his hands on females."

I paused. "So he's just like you, minus the dealer."

"I apologized for that! I heard he's dealing with a lot of females."

"Another you!"

He just looked at me. "I need you to protect Honesty."

"She's grown, but I got her. I'll do some research on him, and you do the same."

"Cool. Keep this between me and you, we don't need Mom to be stressing."

"Okay."

He kissed me on the forehead and went back into Mom's room.

I called my girl, Cali, to see if she heard of Rome.

She answered, and I said, "Good morning, Beautiful."

"Good morning."

"Are you up?"

"Yes. I have to work a couple of hours and then I'm all yours."

That was a good thing because we had both been busy. We hadn't had a chance to make love and cuddle.

"Cool but let me ask you something. You know a guy name Rome?"

"Rome from Lincoln?"

"I guess."

"He's like thirty years old, and he's a big-time drug dealer on the west side.

Very abusive toward women. He has a hand problem, always hitting females. Why, what's up?"

"I think that's the Rome who Honesty is dealing with."

"Oh shit, that's not good."

"I know! I'm going to talk to Hon when she gets out of school. Cali, do you miss me?"

"Hell yeah, those soft lips!"

"I miss you too, and I'll hook up with you later."

"Okay." She hung up.

I headed for the bathroom to get myself together for breakfast.

Chapter 4

By the time I got out of the shower, Mom and Dad were in the kitchen making breakfast: pancakes, eggs, and sausages. Mom looked happy, so I was okay. As long as he didn't hurt her again, I was cool. We all sat together and ate. We put Honesty a plate to the side just as she was walking in saying she was hungry as hell!

I whispered, "We need to talk."

"Fine."

Honesty and I were very close. She gave me advice, and I give it to her. We talked about everything, but this conversation might cause a problem. Still, it was a matter we had to discuss. She knew not to get too loud with me because I would shut her down real quick. When she finished eating, I asked if she was busy.

"No, but later I'm going to meet Rome."

That was my opening. "Speaking of Rome, who is this dude? You been with him for three months and no one in the family has met him. Do he even know we exist?"

"He knows I have a family."

"Does he know you're a twin?"

"No."

"Don't tell him! Honesty, promise me you won't tell him."

She shot me a suspicious look. "Okay, I promise, but I don't understand what the secret is. I want him to meet y'all."

"Just don't tell him. There's a reason, but don't question me about it."

She gave me a side eye. "Okay, Harlem."

I continued. "I know he is dealing drugs. Has he ever asked you to do any or hold anything?"

She looked at me like I was stupid. "No!"

"I know you're damn sure not a virgin anymore."

"How you know?"

"Because you're dealing with a thirty-year-old man. Just make sure you protect yourself."

"Yes, Harlem." She shrugged with a bit of an attitude. "What's with all the questions?"

"Because you're my sister. You're my twin, my other half and I love you to death. I'm concerned about your safety. What did Mom always tell us?"

Honesty replied, "Always protect each other."

"One last question before I leave: has he ever put his hands on you?"

"No!"

I stared at her. "Your dude is known on the streets for hitting women."

"Harlem, I'm good; I promise. If anything was to happen like that, you would be the first to know, and I love you too sis."

I guessed that was her way of telling me no more questions and to get out of her room.

We hugged each other, and I was off to the gym.

Mom let us know she was doing an overnight shift, and Honesty come flying out of her room saying she might be out late with Rome.

Mom said, "You and this Rome!"

Dad kept his mouth shut.

Chapter 5

om said, "I hope you girls are protecting yourselves!"

We looked at each other and said, "Mom!"

"Look at me, both of you: are you?"

"Yes."

Mom had this talk with us several times. She turned to me. "What are your plans for today?"

"I was going to the gym then and coming back here with Cali."

"Okay." She turned to Honesty. "Call one of us and let us know how long you're going to be out."

"For sure." We always told each other our every move to be on the safe side. Hon said, "But for now, I'm going to sleep."

"I'm going to the store to grab some groceries, and your dad is going to head out with me since he has to go to work."

Everyone headed out the door. When I got to the gym, my trainer was waiting for me, looking at the clock. "You're ten minutes late." His name was Rock. He summoned me to do ten squats and twenty pushups.

I thought Rock was hard on me because he had a crush on me and knew I was dealing with a girl. He was always talking slick, saying I needed a stiff one, or a rough man's touch, shit like that. I ignored him because he was a great trainer, one of the best. I did kickboxing, and I was pretty good too. They wanted me in the ring, but I couldn't because I had school and I refused to let this beautiful face get messed up.

By the time I got home, Honesty was getting dressed and Mom was resting before her shift. She had cooked steak, rice, and beans. It was in the oven, and there was dessert in the fridge.

Honesty said, "The dessert is your favorite. Peach cobbler and ice cream."

"Cool."

She shouted, "I'm out!"

I yelled back, "Be safe. I love you!"

"I love you too!"

Mom said, "Ditto, now can I get some rest?"

I laughed. "Yeah, I'm about to shower before Cali gets here."

Chapter 6

I called Cali and told her to pick up a couple of movies.

"Why? We making love all night?"

I laughed. "We can do that."

"Do you want me to grab something to eat?"

"No, my mom cooked and we got dessert."

"Sounds good. I'll see you in a little bit."

A little while later, Dad showed up and asked for Mom. "She's not up yet. She still has a couple hours to relax."

He walked in her room and locked the door. I heard him waking her up. I strained to hear what he was saying. His tone was muffled but it sounded like he was asking to come back.

"No, we're just friends."

He said something else. It sounded like he mentioned this doctor at her job that she was talking to all the time. The doctor kept Mom company at lunch. They went to a Jazz concert, but it was nothing serious.

After a while it got quiet, and then I heard my mom moaning. They were having sex, so I threw my headphones on and laid across the bed and listened to some music. Mom came and tapped on my shoulder. "Good night. I'm leaving. Love you."

I rubbed my eyes. "Where's Dad?"

"He left."

I laid back down until the bell rang. It was Cali. I let her in, then we kissed. "What movies did you pick up?" I asked.

She smiled. "*Stella Got Her Groove Back* and *Waiting To Exhale*. My favorite." I made our plates. We sat in the living room in front of the TV and ate. I finished first, so I started giving her a massage, working my way down to her soft breasts, making her nipples nice and hard. I turned her around and started sucking them, getting her hot and horny. I threw on my strap and we made love on the couch while the movie was going. I enjoyed every part of her soft body. When we finished, we had dessert. Peach cobbler, ice cream, and whipped cream.

Afterward, Cali gave me some information about Rome. Her brother knew him. "He said he's a punk, he only hit on females. He got his ass beat by a couple guys on the west side, young dudes too, but now he's making that paper and everybody wants to get down with him. He got a lot of mouth too, but one of his boys always winds up fighting for him. He gets mad ass though. A lot of females on him. They be throwing the twat at him, but he got a hand problem. My brother asked me if you were dealing with him."

I cut her off. "If I was dealing with him?" I repeated, curling my lip in disgust.

"Chill. I said no, I was asking for a friend. He said, cool, because he would hate to have to go to jail for killing his punk ass. I said, nah big bro, she likes girls, I'm her girlfriend. He said yeah whatever and walked out."

I hesitated for a minute. "This don't look good. This is not the guy for my sister. I gotta think of something quick."

Me and Cali laid back and continued watching the movie while cuddling.

Hon called and said she would be home by three in the morning and that she had already told Mom. "Okay."

Cali set her alarm for six because she had an early shift. We watched TV until we dozed off. The next thing I knew, the damn alarm went off. Cali laid on top of me and said, "I don't want to go. I want to lay with you all day."

"I wish you could, but I got a morning class too and a quiz at nine."

"Bae, focus on this quiz, your other half will be okay."

"I hope so."

She kissed me. "Let's hop in the shower together before your mom comes."

We hurried and by the time we finished and she got dressed and left, my mother came walking in. "You up?"

"Yeah, Cali had a six o'clock shift, but I'm going to lay back down til eight. I have a quiz."

"I'm laying down too. I'm drained. I had a busy night; the ER was full."

When I woke up, Mom was knocked out and as I was about to leave, Honesty came strutting out of her room. "Hey sis, you out?"

"Yes, I am, I have an early morning quiz. What about you?"

"Shit, I'm off til Monday. Where's Mom?"

"Sleep."

"I'm going back to bed too. I had a long night."

"Why was your night long? Were you partying and getting into stuff? Hon, you can party all you want but you better stay focused on school."

"Dang, I know Harlem!"

"Dang, my ass! Love you."

"Love you Harlem, have a good day."

I left to ace this quiz and get back home. My college grades were A's and Bs. Both of us always had high GPA's. The quiz was like a test, long as hell but I was able to finish on time. I went and got some extra credit from the professor just in case I missed any assignments.

After leaving school, I went to the gym for a while did some shadowboxing. I kicked the bag around for a while, then went and brought my baby some lunch. Cali's favorite meal was shrimp and broccoli with extra sauce. I brought me some ribs, wings and beef fried rice and some lo mein, enough for Mom and Honesty for lunch.

Chapter 7

Whn I got home, Mom and Hon were knocked out. I woke them up by yelling, "Lunch time!"

Mom said, "Harlem, why are you so loud?"

Honesty said, "Yes, Harlem, why are you so loud?"

"Because I want y'all to eat with me and then y'all can go back to sleep. We all can eat in Mom's big old bed."

Mom said, "Y'all are always welcome to lay in my bed."

We ate and laid in the bed with our mommy like when we were younger. We slept so long we lost track of time, shit it was evening. Mom said she was off since she did an overnight shift, so decided I was gonna hang with her, until she said she had other plans.

"We can hang out as soon as I get back from dinner with the doctor."

Honesty said, "The doctor!"

Mom said, "Yes, the doctor."

Hon said, "Harlem, I will be back in a little while," as she was running her shower water.

"Go ahead leave me by myself!"

They started laughing. Mom said, "We're coming back."

"I got extra homework anyway."

Honesty yelled, "Can you go over mine in the folder in my laptop to make sure it's good?"

"I will check it out."

Honesty always left the bathroom door cracked while she took showers like she was scared and shit, so I busted through and pulled the shower curtain back to ask her for the code to the laptop. She jumped, which was what I was aiming for, but that was when I saw the big ass bruise on her leg. I immediately grew angry. "What the fuck is that?"

Mom heard me. "Who just cursed in my house!"

"Sorry Mom, it slipped out."

"Don't let it happen again because my hand is going to slip right across your lips!"

Honesty looked scared. "Shoosh!"

"Don't shoosh me, where did you get that?"

"The other night I had a couple of drinks and fell on the stairs. It must have happened then. I never noticed it."

I stared at her. "You better not be lying."

"Harlem, have I ever lied to you? I don't keep nothing from you."

I just looked, closed the shower curtain and kept my mouth shut. Now I was worried.

She came out of the bathroom and I was sitting at the desk. She put her arms around my neck and said, "Sis, I'm good. Stop worrying so much, God got us."

"Tell me one thing Mom told us when we were nine."

She sighed. "Never let a man put his hands on you. If he does, it's time to cut him loose. Never let a man disrespect you, call you names or put you down in any type of way."

"And what else, Hon?"

"She said we should always protect each other."

"Okay, so are you good?"

"Yes." She kissed the top of my head. "I'll be back in a little while." Mom was getting all dressed up for her doctor friend. She looked amazing and smelled good. She was all ready to go and her phone rang, He was outside sitting in his Benz. He got out and opened the car door for her. She found a gentleman, handsome and polite.

Once they left, I started checking Honesty's paper. She had a couple errors I fixed, now she was good. I started my extra credit assignments then talked to Cali on her break. She said she might pull a double because she wanted us to go on a vacation for her birthday during spring break, either Miami, Vegas, or the Bahamas.

I hung up and got bored, so I called my friend Kelsey to see what she was up to. She was running to the mall, so she asked me to ride with her. "I'll spin by and get you in about thirty minutes."

Kelsey knew everything about the streets. She liked partying and having fun. I knew her since high school. Cali got a little jealous about our friendship, but I knew for a fact Kelsey would always have my back. She pulled up and I hopped in the car and asked her what was at the mall.

"I need some jeans and Timberland boots. I'm going to the club with my boo so I'm planning to shoplift."

I rolled my eyes then changed the subject. "Kelsey, do you be on the west side?"

"Yeah, I run through there every now and then. My family lives over there, why what's up?"

I cut to the chase. "Do you know a Rome?"

Her facial expression changed. "Woman-beater Rome? Hell yeah, he's a bitch, a big time drug dealer. He makes mad loot and he got mad girls on him but he's not a fighter, he just hit females. Why, he did something to you? 'Cause I can get him fucked up real quick."

"Nah, I just hear people talking about him, saying he got money and he hits women, shit like that."

"If you need me for anything, let me know, you know I got your back."

"Cool."

By the time Kelsey dropped me back off, Honesty still wasn't home.

Mom was back. She brought us a big platter of food home. She was in a good mood. She must have enjoyed herself with the good old doctor. "Did your dad call or pop up?"

"No, but he will."

"Did your other half come home or call?"

"No."

She yawned. "Well, it's after ten. In another hour we will give her a call." She went to take a shower and told me to eat something. She brought shrimp scampi with steak and it was delicious. I sat in front of the TV watching *The Women of Brewster Place*.

When Mom got out of the shower, she joined me. She loved that movie. While were sitting there, she called Hon and the answering machine kept coming on.

"Harlem, try and call your sister."

Mom was getting worried. She worried about us all the time, but mostly Honesty because she knew how soft and friendly she was. "If your other half don't call or walk in this door by one, she's going to feel my wrath."

"Mom, it's okay. She'll call or come in. She always does."

"Her dealing with this Rome guy, I don't think it's a good idea. Now I have to put a stop to it because she's not following the rules."

"Mom, I'll talk to her when she gets in."

"Good, because I'm tired and going to lay across the bed."

I waited up for Honesty, but her phone still was going to voicemail.

She walked in at one forty-five and went straight to her room.

I cut the TV off and followed.

She was tipsy and smelled liked alcohol.

"Hon, what are you doing?"

"Enjoying life, Harlem Night."

I took her clothes off and noticed a bruise on her left arm. I stared at it in shock. "You know what? Get some sleep and we are going to talk in the morning! Do not leave out the damn door until you see me and Mommy."

"Okay, love you, Sis."

"Yeah, love you too."

I put the cover on her and left out, then checked on Mom.

I laid in my bed thinking this guy Rome was hitting on my sister, but she was so in love she was letting it happen.

Chapter 8

It was morning and I heard Mom calling Honesty to her room. Honesty was in the bathroom vomiting. I got up to check on her. "Hon, what the hell were you drinking?"

"Gin, vodka, a little bit of everything."

"This is not you. What are you trying to prove to Rome, that you're that ride or die chick?"

"No."

I wasn't convinced. "It's something, because you don't drink. Straighten up and brush your teeth. Your breath smells like straight alcohol. And go talk to Mom because she's mad as hell!"

Honesty held her temples in her palms. "I know, my head hurts."

"I will get you something for it." A couple minutes later I heard Mom yelling and Hon crying. I didn't know what she said but Honesty felt her wrath for the first time. Mom always did the talking and Dad did the yelling.

Now it was my turn to check Honesty because she was fucking up big time. Me and Hon always got whatever we wanted from our parents: money, clothes, food... We even got cars, Honda Accords in different colors. But now Honesty had hooked up with her first piece of dick and she was tripping over him. I went in the room and she was laying on the bed pouting like a baby.

"Don't pout now, sit up."

She sucked her teeth. "Leave me alone."

"No, what's up with you?"

"Mommy said I gotta leave Rome alone since I can't follow her rules and I'm not staying focused."

"She's right! You're trying to fit in with a crowd that's not even your type. You never drank anything besides milk, Kool-Aid, or damn water. I'm the drinker, gambler and all that type of shit. Then you're not checking in and that's the number one rule. Lastly, I'm going to ask you one more time where the fuck that bruise come from on your arm. I don't want to hear you fell."

Honesty's face fell. "I was dancing with one of Rome's friends and he got mad and grabbed me and said don't disrespect him, and that's when it must have happened. Harlem, he didn't hit me!"

I didn't believe her. This was bad. "If you're lying, Honesty, and I find out, you are going to have to fight me and Rome is a dead man walking, I promise you."

"Please don't tell Mom."

"I'm not, but you got to do one thing. I want you take some time away from Rome to get back on track. Even though Mom said stay away, I know you won't."

"Fine, I'll let him know we need to give each other some space."

"We love you. What's your plans for today?"

"Shit, Mom told me I better not walk out her door today. Anyway, my head is pounding."

"Mom's on the phone with Dad," I warned.

"Shit! I better be prepared, 'cause he's coming."

"I'm heading to the gym to box a couple of rounds." I closed her room door and went in Mom's room and flopped on the bed. "Did you ground Honesty?"

"I sure did. Did you want a day?"

"Nope, but you do know we're too old to be grounded, right?"

"Not in my house. If you follow my rules like you supposed to you won't get grounded. I raised y'all to be polite, respectful, not to talk back, to say your prayers before meals and bedtime and to follow the rules."

"Yes, Ma'am, you definitely raised us right."

"Now look at y'all beautiful, mature young women. Amen to that." She kissed me on the forehead and said, "Let me go check on my drunken baby and give her something for the hangover."

I laughed. "I'm heading to the gym, be back in a little while."

My dad was coming to the house because Mom kept no secrets from him when it came to us. If there was a problem, we all figured it out together. Right now, Hon had a problem. She was in love, which was a good thing, just with the wrong guy. She deserved better.

Chapter 9

By the time I got back home, my dad and mom were sitting in the living room. "Where's Honesty?"

Dad said, "In her room pouting."

"Why?"

"Because the only part of outside she'll be seeing is when she's going to school for a week."

"Are y'all doing this because y'all want her to stay away from Rome? When her week is up, what do you think is going to happen? There has to be a better solution."

Dad said, "That is the solution, Einstein."

"Okay." I wasn't going to argue with him. I looked at Mom and went to check on my other half. She was asleep so I laid next to her and held her until I dozed off.

A couple hours later, Mom came and woke us up. Honesty reached for her phone. She had a lot of missed calls from Rome. His name said *Bae* in her contacts. He was probably wondering why she wasn't answering his calls or texts.

Mom came back in the room and asked if we wanted to make a run with her to the bank and then grab some dinner because she was doing an overnight shift. We said yes, because we wanted Red Lobster.

"Let's go."

We got dressed and left. We made our stop and went off to eat. Mom said we could order whatever we wanted. Hon's greedy self ordered lobster, shrimps, and salad. I had king clusters and salad. Mom did steak, salad, and biscuits. We ate until we got full then left.

She brought Dad some food too. "I'm going to drop you girls off with your dad's food, then head to work." She asked if I was going anywhere.

"No, because Cali is working late so I'm staying in."

"Good, you can hang with your sister since she's grounded."

Honesty sucked her teeth. "Come on, Mommy."

"You heard what your dad said."

Hon walked off stomping. Mom said, "That means no good night? No kiss or nothing?"

I gave her a hug and said, "Good night, love you."

Hon turned around. "Good night, Mom. Love you."

Mom watched as we entered the house and then drove off.

Hon's phone was steady going off. I went to my room to watch TV. A couple minutes later, she peeked in my room and said, "Harlem Night, I'm running to the corner store, I'll be right back."

"Hon, five minutes, you got it?"

My phone rang. It was Mom. "Is Honesty alright?"

"She's fine, she ran to the corner store. I told her she had five minutes."

Mom sucked her teeth. "She had to find some way to get out the door. Call me when she gets back."

I wound up watching the *The Equalizer 2* on bootleg and I was so into it I lost track of time. I started yelling, "Hey Hon!" because I hadn't seen her since she peeked in my room to go to the store and that was like a half hour ago. I yelled her name again, no answer. I got up and walked through the house to check her room. She wasn't there. Damn, I didn't want to call Mom because she would start worrying. I grabbed my phone and dialed Honesty. She picked up.

"Where the hell are you?"

"I'm coming now."

"It doesn't take a half hour to go to the corner store." I heard moaning in the background and it was a man. "Hon, please tell me you're not with Rome and y'all fucking."

"Give me a minute and I'll be there."

I heard him say he was about to cum. She hung up on me. She had snuck off to get some dick. I was beyond pissed, not because she was having sex but because she lied and said she was going to the store. She knew I wasn't going to snitch on her because she had covered for me many times while we were growing up.

My sister had twenty minutes to get her ass home and I was going to let her have it.

Chapter 10

As I sat there rocking back and forth and watching the rest of *Equalizer*, Honesty came flying through the door. "I'm here!"

I looked at her. "You snuck out to get a piece of dick, are you serious? So Rome is more important than your family."

"No!"

"So, what is it? Talk to me sis."

"He kept calling and texting saying he needed to see me. I told him I couldn't. He said I must have been with his boy Wisdom, 'cause he wasn't around either. I told him I needed a little space so I could focus on school. He asked if I was fucking Wisdom. I told him I wasn't. He said we're always in each other's faces. He said I needed to prove I wasn't with Wisdom. So I did. When I got there, he wanted some sex so when you called, we were in the middle of having sex. I'm sorry sis, I just wanted to prove him wrong."

I couldn't believe my ears. I didn't know where to start. "What did he say about you needing your space?"

"He said there is no space."

I knew it. "This is going to be a problem."

Mom called and asked what we were doing.

Hon begged me not to tell. I rolled my eyes. "We're watching TV."

"Okay, just checking in. Love you girls."

"We love you too." I hung up.

Hon said, "Thanks sis," and walked to the bathroom to run her shower water. I was so pissed that I walked in my room and closed the door. I had so much on my mind I couldn't even get into the rest of the movie.

When morning came, I got up and ate some cereal, checked in on Mom, showered and headed to class. Hon had a class too, but I didn't wait for her. After my fourth class, Cali called my phone and wanted to have lunch, so I met her at the pizza place and told her about Hon.

She gasped. "Not miss goodie! Give her some time; she'll get over him."

"I hope she does."

"What are you going to do after school?"

"Maybe go to the gym."

"I get off early so we can hang out at my spot for a while then I'll going back to work to do some overtime."

"Cool." Cali was going to help me relieve some of this stress. I went back to school and walked right into Hon.

She smirked, but I could tell by her eyes she felt guilty. "Harlem Night, are you mad at me?"

"No, I'm upset with you."

"I apologized to you for last night."

"Honesty, you just don't get it. You lied! If something would have happened to you, I would not have known. We're supposed to protect each other, and that guy you're dealing with is a woman beater. I know you know all this shit you've been doing is making it hard for me to trust you. Yes, you're grown and you don't want us to know your every move, but when you pull a stunt like that, anything could have happened and the only information I would've had was that you said you were going to the corner store."

Her face scrunched like she was about to cry. "It won't happen again. Besides I'm giving him some space."

"We will see! I got to get to my last class. Love you, sis."

"Love you too, Harlem Night."

Chapter 11

I left school and didn't feel like going to the gym. I went home instead, and Dad was eating lunch with Mom. I grabbed a piece of fruit out of the fridge and went in my room to start my homework and wait for Cali to come get me.

Hon had a few more classes than me.

Dad knocked on my door and asked, "Has Hon been outside besides going to school?"

"No."

He studied me. "'Cause if I find out she has, I'm going to whoop her ass and kill him."

"Dad, she's been home, so don't go killing anyone."

He stood solid. "I don't mind going to jail for my girls."

"Well, we mind."

"Just checking." He closed the door. I didn't need my dad to get in any trouble that was going to cost him his job or life. I was going to handle this one on my own. Hon walked in and gave Mom a kiss and Dad a fake wave. She must have been mad at him for grounding her.

"That's all I get?" he asked.

She didn't respond.

He said to Mom, "They're not that grown. They still can get their asses whooped."

Mom said, "You're not putting your hands on my girls!"

"They are mine too! Let them keep trying me."

"Watson, let's change the subject because I said what I had to say."

He looked at her. "Oh yeah?" He brought up the doctor Mom was seeing. "You thought I wouldn't find out? I hear about everything."

Mom was unbothered. "Remember, we're divorced. Me and you just have kids together and decided to remain friends because of them."

"But we have sex too."

"And it's just sex."

"Are you fucking this doctor?"

"Not that it's any of your business what I'm doing, but it's only you. Can I ask you the same?"

He got quiet.

"Watson, we agreed that we will only talk about the girls, not who's fucking who."

"You're right, but you do know I'm still in love with you."

Honesty came out of her room asking if she could leave out this boring house today. I got saved by the bell, Cali was here. She came and gave everybody a hug and I grabbed my stuff. "Mom, I'll be back before you head to work. Dad, I'll see you later, and Hon, enjoy this boring house!"

Honesty said, "Come on, Mom and Dad! It's been two days."

Mom said, "Talk to your dad. I gave you one day, and he gave you the week."

Dad interjected. "No. You have five more days. There are seven days in a week, not two." She walked out mumbling, "Watch me leave out this house."

I went to spend time with my baby and we made love til it was time for me to leave and her to go back to work. I felt stress free for the moment. I loved her soft body on me, her lips touching mine, her hands massaging me, sucking on her nice plum shaped breasts, and the sweet smell of perfume she wore. She was my everything.

Chapter 12

When I got home it was late. Mom had already left for work. She was doing an overnight so she could be off tomorrow to relax. It was a little after midnight so I went in my room and changed into my night clothes. I called my mom and told her I was home. "Okay, check in on your sister because she was upset earlier when your dad told her she had five more days."

"Okay. Love you."

"Ditto."

Once I got situated, I knocked on Honesty's door. She didn't answer, so I turned the knob and looked in. She wasn't there. I called her name because our house was kind of big. Still no answer. She had snuck out. I called her phone and it went to voicemail, so I kept calling. After the fourth time, she answered. I could hear a bunch of people and music in the background. "Honesty, where are you?"

"Harlem, I'm good. I'll be there in a couple of hours. I'm chilling with Rome."

"So you snuck out to be with this bum ass guy Rome?"

"Harlem Night, chill. I will be home before Mom gets home. She will never know."

"Yes, she will, because I'm calling her and Dad right now."

"No, Harlem! I'm leaving right now, I just wanted to see him, and he needed to see me he said."

"You have thirty minutes to walk in this door."

"Okay cool, I'm on my way."

I hung up and started pacing through the house, all worried and shit. If I smoked cigarettes, I probably would have smoked a half a pack by now. I kept watching the clock. I sat and stared at the front door, praying she walked through it, but I had this feeling that something was wrong.

After thirty minutes passed, I said, "Let me give her an extra ten minutes." I waited and when I went to dial her number, I got cut off by Cali. I answered and said, "Bae, I'm going to call you right back. Hon done snuck out the house to go see Rome."

Cali said, "Harlem baby, you need to come to the hospital now and call your Mom and Dad. Rome has beaten Hon up real bad."

I dropped the phone threw on my clothes, hopped in my car and headed to the hospital.

Cali greeted me and said, "This guy named Wisdom brought her in." She pointed at him. Wisdom approached me. He looked nervous as he told me what happened. "When we were at the club, Honesty was trying to go home and Rome wouldn't let her. He started pushing her toward the back, telling her she wasn't going anywhere. He grabbed her and she broke loose. He got mad and hit her and she hit him back, then he started fighting her. Once I noticed him hitting her like a man, I started fighting Rome. Did you call your Mom?"

I was in a daze. "No, I dropped my phone in the house. Is she alright?"

Cali spoke up. "The nurse said she's in a coma, she has some blows to the head."

I started crying.

Cali was on her phone. "Mom's on her way, and she'll call Dad."

Fifteen minutes later, Dad and Mom came running in the hospital asking where was their baby. The lady at the front desk stopped them, took them to the side and explained that she was in a coma from blows to the head and had a fractured rib, five stitches inside her lip and a broken hand.

My mom started crying. She asked what happened, and I said, "When I got home and called you, I checked on her like you said and she wasn't in her room. I called her and she didn't answer as usual. After the fourth call she answered and said she was on her way home. She went to see Rome. The next thing I know, Cali called and said we need to come to the hospital."

My dad was fucking pissed. "I'm going to kill him!" He went storming out the door.

"Mom, get Dad before he winds up in jail!"

She went running after him.

The guy Wisdom was still there. I thanked him for bringing my sister to the hospital. He just stared and said, "There are two of you."

"Yes but do me a favor. Please don't tell anyone right now."

"You got my word, but y'all look exactly alike."

"Thanks."

Mom finally calmed Dad down and they came back inside.

The police came and took a report and one of them was my dad's friend. They put out a warrant for Rome and my dad went to the precinct to put a restraining order against him, so he couldn't come near her. We stayed and they let us see her. We stood around her and Mom said a healing prayer. Wisdom left but he said our secret was safe with him.

Chapter 13

Now it was time for revenge. Once Honesty was good, it was on. I promised this motherfucker would never hit another female again.

We took turns staying the night with Honesty.

Most of the time, Cali was there with her. Mom took some of her vacation days, so she could be there when Honesty woke up. After a week, my other half came through. She was out of the coma. She opened her eyes and was so happy to see all of us standing there: me, Mom, Dad and Cali. She couldn't talk. The nurse said it was going to take a while. She was looking for her phone, but I had taken it home to charge it because it was dead. She had a bunch of missed calls and texts from Rome apologizing.

I erased his number and broke her phone so she couldn't read them or get in touch with him. When she was able to talk, she mumbled and asked for her phone. She talked funny because of the stitches inside her lip. I told her it was broken. I tried to charge it, but it was all cracked up. She asked how she got to the hospital.

I said, "Wisdom."

She tried to smile.

She took my phone and texted my mom and dad saying she was sorry for disobeying them. She would never do it again.

Mom said, "This is the reason we have rules, so things like this won't happen. If you would have stayed in like your dad said, you wouldn't be in the hospital. Am I right or wrong!"

Hon mumbled, "You're right."

Dad said, "You're alive and that's the only thing that matters right now, but his ass is mine."

"Dad!"

"Harlem, I can't give him a pass on this one. Not one of mine."

I walked my dad out of the room. Cali was looking at me. I lowered my tone as I spoke to him. "Dad, I got this. I promise you."

He registered what I was saying. "Hell no! I don't want you to get hurt."

"Dad, I'm not. I got this. Did you get that restraining order?"

"Yeah, I got it on both of y'all because he might think you are her. My cop friend said to get it on both of y'all. It's at Mom's house on top of the chest in her room and there's one here at the hospital."

"Cool, just leave the rest up to me."

My father spoke his next words slowly. "I'm not going to promise you that I'm not going to kill this bastard, but I'll give you a couple days."

We walked back into the room. The nurse came to check Honesty. She explained to her that she had a concussion, a fractured rib in two spots, a broken hand, and five stitches inside her lip and a bruise under her right eye. She would be in the hospital for another week. That gave me time to set shit up.

Later that night, me and Cali went to her place. Mom stayed with Hon. Dad went to work and said he would be back in the early morning.

I told Cali I had a plan and I was going to need her help. I needed a couple of bandages for my hand and some makeup to make a bruise under my eye.

She cocked her head at me. "What are you about to do, act like Honesty? Hell no!"

"Cali, I have to do this. You know I can defend myself."

"Bae, what if he has something on him? A weapon."

"That's a chance I'm going to have to take. I'm good, just don't tell my mom. She will freak the fuck out."

"Okay, but Bae, please be careful."

"I need a prepaid phone."

"I can get you one tomorrow."

"Get a cheap one with like twenty minutes on it."

"I will have everything by tomorrow."

"Thanks, and don't worry. I got this." I kissed her on the forehead while we laid and watched TV.

When I got home in the morning, Mom was in the shower getting herself together so she could head back to the hospital. Dad was already there. He went as soon as he got off from work.

"Tell Hon I'll be there later after class."

Mom said, "Okay," and came out of the bathroom. She gave me a kiss as she walked past. I headed for the shower so I could make it to my morning class and I wanted to head to the gym for a while. I missed a couple of days since Hon got hurt.

Cali gave me a call around lunch time and said to meet her at the pizza spot. When I got there, we ate, and she had everything I asked for.

"When is all this going down?"

"Today!"

I could tell she was shocked. "Whatever you do, please be careful."

"Okay Bae; don't worry. What time you get off?"

"Midnight."

"Okay, you can stay at my house. I will let Mom know. I'm going to the hospital with you to sit with Honesty for a while then I'm going to head back home."

"One question, what's the phone for?"

"I'm going to call Rome from it, break it and throw it away in the dumpster down the street."

I walked in and Hon was doing much better. She was eating a little, but it hurt because of the stitches. Cali had some patients she had to check on. While she did that, I called my girl Kelsey.

She answered on the third ring. "What's up?"

I got right to it. "I need you to do me a favor."

"Anything for you."

"I need you to go to the Westside."

"Heading that way now to see my cousin."

"Get word out to one of Rome's guys that the chick he beat up is out of the hospital."

"What chick?"

"I will explain later, I promise. Just make sure he gets the message. Tell a couple of his boys."

"Okay, I'll hit my cousin right now and tell him to put the word out. He hangs around them sometimes."

"Cool, good looking out."

"You better put me down."

"Got you." I waited another hour and kissed everybody and said I would be back in a little while. I had homework I had to get done. Mom said, "Love you," then Dad said it, and Honesty tried, but I understood.

I found Cali and told her to listen out for her phone.

"Okay."

"Give me about thirty to forty minutes."

I got home and put the bandage on my hand, a bruise under my right eye with the makeup, put on a tank top since it was easy to rip, and some tights. I called Rome's phone from the prepaid phone Cali gave me. He didn't pick up. I waited five minutes and called again. No answer. Two minutes later, he called back and said, "Who's this?"

"Honesty!"

"What's up, baby? I been trying to reach out to you. Whose phone are you calling me from?"

"Mine; you broke my other phone."

"Sorry. I heard you were home. I didn't mean to hit you, but I was mad you wanted to leave."

"Where you at?"

"I'm at home. Come see me, I want some of your sex. You be nice and wet."

"I can't; no one's home and I lost my keys."

"Shit, can I slide through real quick?"

That was just what I wanted to hear. "Real quick? Where you at?"

"On my way back from picking up my shit."

"Don't bring no drugs in my house!"

"Why would I do that? I keep my shit in the trunk and my guns I leave under my seat."

"How long you going to be, because we have to make it quick."

"Where's your parents?"

"My mom's at work and my dad don't live with us but he's at work too."

"Give me your address."

I gave it to him and he said, "I'm right around the way. Be there in ten minutes."

I ran to the corner and threw the prepaid phone in the dumpster and waited. I was a little nervous, but this was for my sister. I didn't play about my mom or my other half.

After stretching and pacing for a couple minutes, I saw him pull up. I cracked the door open, then called the police from my cell phone and told them I saw the guy my sister was attacked by walking toward my house. "I'm her twin and we have a restraining order against him! I'm the only one home."

Rome pushed the door open and started calling my name.

I came out and stared him down.

He smiled, but when he heard what I had to say, it was on. "Rome, it's over with us. I don't want to be bothered no more. I'm too good of a person and you're very abusive."

His entire facial expression changed. "What? You're never getting rid of me!" He grabbed me and tried to kiss me.

I slapped him, and he slapped me back and busted my lip. He ripped my tank top halfway off and that was when I got right. I hit him with a combination, busted his lip and nose.

He came charging at me. I drop-kicked him in the nuts and he fell down.

"You like beating on women?"

I hit him with another combination and kept throwing blows to his face and split his eyes.

He got up and I started hitting him in his ribs back to back. "This for my sister, Honesty!" I hit him with an uppercut.

He went down, and I kicked him down the stairs right into the cops coming up.

"Miss, are you okay?"

I faked like I was hysterical. "Yes, he thought I was my twin sister. She's still in the hospital. He walked in the house. I thought I locked the door! He threatened me, saying don't make me go to my car and get my gun out from under the seat! He was trying to rape me. He ripped my shirt off and we started fighting." I threw a tremble in my tone during my story, hoping the cops believed me.

They called two ambulances, one for him and one for me.

Once I was out of earshot, I called Cali and said, "Bae, I did it. I'm on my way."

When I got to the hospital, Mom and Dad had heard they were bringing a man and woman in. They didn't know it was me. Cali told them to come to the front. They saw them pushing a guy in. Cali said, "That's Rome!"

I came walking in behind him.

Mom and Dad ran to me and said, "Harlem, what did you do!"

"Self-defense. I beat his ass. He fucked with the right twin!"

Mom said, "Watch your mouth."

I got checked out by the emergency room doctor. I had a busted lip and a broken finger. I was good.

He had twenty stitches on his face, a broken nose, a busted lip, a missing tooth, a broken rib and a concussion.

Inside his car they found two guns, marijuana and heroin and he violated his restraining order.

The day Rome was sentenced, Honesty announced that her and Wisdom were dating. He had been stopping by the house to see her and was always respectful. Word on the street was that Rome got another beatdown while he was in jail due to him.

Rome didn't deserve my sister, but Wisdom seemed like the one.

Still, I kept my eyes on him. I still didn't play about my other half.

LADIES, IF YOU'RE IN AN ABUSIVE RELATIONSHIP, GET OUT! DON'T WAIT TIL IT'S TOO LATE. EVEN IF IT'S VERBAL ABUSE, THAT LEADS INTO PHYSICAL ABUSE.

IF YOU'RE IN THIS SITUATION, TELL SOMEONE. DO NOT TOLERATE ABUSE FROM ANYONE...

I AM MY SISTER'S PROTECTOR.

SINCERELY, CHONTAE COOK

Books By Chontae Cook

<u>Chontae's Thoughts: Poems of Life, Friendship, & Blessings</u>

<u>Love, Betrayal, & Hidden Secrets: A Collection of Short Stories and Poems</u>

<u>Undercover: I'm in</u>

<u>Undercover 2: Secrets and Lies</u>

<u>Undercover 3: Trust and Revenge</u>

<u>Undercover 4: Someone's Watching</u>

<u>Divas on the Run</u>